FROM NATURE

Johns Hopkins: Poetry and Fiction   John T. Irwin, General Editor

FROM

poems by *THOMAS CARPER*

NATURE

THE JOHNS HOPKINS UNIVERSITY PRESS
BALTIMORE AND LONDON

This book has been brought to publication with the generous assistance of the Albert Dowling Trust.

04 03 02 01 00 99 98 97 96 95   5 4 3 2 1

The Johns Hopkins University Press
2715 North Charles Street
Baltimore, Maryland 21218-4319
The Johns Hopkins Press Ltd., London

LIBRARY OF CONGRESS CATALOGING-IN-PUBLICATION DATA

Carper, Thomas.
    From nature : poems / by Thomas Carper.
        p.   cm. — (Johns Hopkins, poetry and fiction)
    ISBN 0-8018-5208-0 (alk. paper)
    I. Title.   II. Series.
PS3553.A7625F76 1995
811′.54—dc20   95-15478

A catalog record for this book is available from the British Library.

For Janet again

Contents

MEMORIALS

PAINTERS, MUSICIANS, WRITERS

SHORT STORIES

FOUR SEQUENCES

MEMORIALS

Photograph of the Father and His Baby Boy

His past is hung upon the wall, with seals
Of two diplomas visible in the shade.
Undoubtedly the youthful father feels
The tightly delicate fist his son has made
Around an extended finger, and the weight
Of the small head laid back upon his chest.
The photograph would have us meditate
Upon that grasp, those papers, and the rest:
The father's half-closed lids; the open book
Placed on the table close beside the chair
When, after she had brought him in, he took
His son into his arms; and then the stare
Of the child's eyes that seem to fix their sight
On a faceted glass doorknob filled with light.

Birthday Moon Fear

"It's beautiful." She touched me. But her touch
This time was useless. She said, "It's the moon,"
Again, as if the simple words were such
As could remove a deepening fear that soon
Would show in lines my sudden tears would trace
While I stood crying, staring at the stark
Outlines of branches cracking the creamy face
That stared back at me blankly through the dark.
"It's moonlight. You will learn to love it." She
Turned my small shoulders, led me to a chair
And brought the cake, and had me blow the three
Thin candles out. I calmed, though half-aware
That earth's bright moon, for me, would coldly stay
No intimate distance, but light-years away.

Funny Face

His muscles tensed like clockwork when he heard
A big one say, "Now make your funny face."
Setting himself to please, without a word
He'd put his twisted puckerings in place.
Big ones would be delighted. They would clap,
Call him a little wonder, and then turn
To grown-up talk. He'd slide from Mother's lap,
Cross the broad porch, escaping their concern,
And go down to his sandbox in the yard
Where he could listen to them overhead
While making hills and holes. Once, having starred
Again, he winced when someone sternly said,
"Tom will do anything to get a laugh,"
In tones that sounded like an epitaph.

Watching the Storm

The boy sits on the filing cabinet
In Father's study, dangling his feet
Over the edge, and leaning toward the wet
World beyond the window. Down the street
A deluge swirls, but he is safely dry,
And comforted to hear the steam pipes groan.
Though waves of rain sweep through a darkened sky,
He has no fear of being here alone.
Around the study, shelves that bear the books
In which his father's faith is written down
Reach almost to the ceiling. The boy looks
At all that weight and learning. With a frown
He turns back to the storm, the street, the flow
Of water going where it has to go.

The Nap

He'd order us out: "Now you should go and play."
So into sweaty afternoons we went,
Leaving the cool house of our holiday
To adult sleep. But what those exiles meant
Was our not mattering. He would set his jaw
Too firmly when his seeming-gentle voice
Wisped out upon us, laying down the law,
His small eyes saying, "Children have no choice."
Condemned, then, to three hours of comradeship
With friends I had not chosen, I would work
At being the dutiful boy, and try to slip
Into indifference. Yet an emotional murk
Dissolved one day while we were forced to wait
To get back in: here I was learning hate.

Connections

We had some wires and tools, and a vocation.
We'd make our mark. Inventing for ourselves
The Carper-White Electrical Association,
We stocked with parts a closetful of shelves.
Our plan was to fix lamps; communicate
With old transmitters ordered through the mail;
Run cables through a woodlot and create
A string of telephones along the trail.
We advertised by nailing to a tree
Beside my house a two-foot plywood square
With brightly painted letters—C-W-E-
And A—to tell the world that we were there.
Those early boyhood projects still are mine:
Making connections, putting up a sign.

The Duet

Like a boy actor in an early play,
Dressed in a gown, he was a pretty bride
For me, who in a stiff last-century way
Walked her across the wide stage by my side,
Singing a southern tune: "That's where my heart
Is turning ever." Moving in the light
That kept us in its circle, set apart
From other men and boys, initial fright
Ebbed as our voices made their blended sound
The domination of the darkened space
Above the audience, as though it found
A home there, an enduring dwelling place—
Which, at the last note, vanished. Then, a pause
Said we would soon be bowing to applause.

Wrestling

Real boys, of course, played football, but a few
Outcasts, like me, each autumn were brought in
To get our dose of exercise and do
Long, sweaty workouts wrestling in the gym.
Some liked their grappling through the grim routines;
Rail-skinny types — mine — and the chunky fat
Usually hated the semisexual scenes
Where hammerlocks would pin us to the mat.
And yet it was decreed that we should be
A team, and challenge other teams, and go
To other schools where the futility
Of all our straining could be put on show.
I was an image of our worst — beneath
The opposition, struggling to breathe.

How Mother Is

The people at the Care Center are kind,
And, as we live long distances away,
They send brief notes and photos that remind
Us of her irreversible decay.
We're glad to see her face at eighty-one
Still young, though hands are frighteningly thin,
With every bluish vein, and joint, and bone
Visible through a glassy sheath of skin.
We're told her eyes stay focused when they meet
Another's eyes, and that she seems content;
When nurses help her up onto her feet
She "walks at all times with encouragement."
She starts no conversation, although while
Another speaks, she does not cease to smile.

Her Handbag

She picks it up and shuffles toward the door.
The handbag's straps are gone. The metal clasp
Is broken. Hardly useful anymore,
It's one thing she can keep within her grasp.
She makes her way into the dining hall
To eat with men and women such as she,
Declining people, who cannot recall
The plenitude that once was memory.
Sometimes inside her handbag silverware —
Forks, knives, and spoons — is gently stored away,
Then "loaned" to nurses who are sure it's there,
Though everyone's most careful not to say,
"Now, let us have the bag," for she'll say, "No,"
And hug it close and will not let it go.

Step by Step

In whispers Grandmother would count the stairs
When going slowly up them, though ashamed
When others overheard her unawares,
Thinking some mental failure might be blamed.
Yet she had counted since a child; perhaps
An instinct, something private and her own,
Had given her the habit—not a lapse,
But an unfailing way to make things known.
And now she's gone. And now I number, too:
The syllables in lines (most often, ten),
And fourteen lines desiring to ring true;
And, yes, the hours that won't come back again,
The years . . . the step and step of life, amounting
To one long stairway where I'm climbing, counting.

A Four-Crossing Run

Little River gathers in a lowland
Between Pease Mountain and Day Hill, then runs
Three miles through marshes northward into Cornish,
Loops to the mill pond, drops over the dam
To ooze or rush, depending on the season,
Into the Ossipee. My run today
Begins at Fiddle Lane, and my first crossing
Is on Route 25, over the bridge
Where traffic slows and turns, and where some schoolkids
Are watching water fall into the gorge.
Going through the Town Woods, past the houses
On King Street, through a grove above the pond,
I make a second crossing on a culvert
And come out into sunshine for an easy
Upgrade, then that long and welcome slope
A quarter of a mile to crossing three.
The flowers are out in gardens by the roadside,
And from a cleared field cows look blandly at me.
Children have left a wagon in a driveway;
A black retriever, straining at his chain,
Protests my passing, but I pass, then over
Little River, where the water ripples,

Catching the light. Now, southward from the village,
The houses stop. The backbones of the hills
Rise behind the tracts of marsh, where water
Lies at or near the level of the land.
I find myself, here on a final bridge,
Slowing my pace, looking from left to right
Over the stunted trees and spongy boundaries
That guide the flow that passes under me
To mark the outer limit of my running.
I have gone far enough. Now, with the current,
I turn and follow Little River home.

A Ball of Surprises

They were rare and precious. I was given
One—it was my birthday. I remember
Its roundness, bigger than my two small hands,
And blueness, like the water in a pool.
Its tag said, "Happy Birthday. Begin Here."
So with a little tug the blue came loose
In a thin strip and started its unwinding.
I hadn't unwound far before I found it,
The first surprise: a tiny workable whistle.
Then, as the paper spiraled to my feet,
Two gifts at once: a silvery knife and rake.
This was exciting. Though the ball got smaller,
Presents came thick and fast: a book, a car,
A ring—it seemed it might go on forever,
With blueness piling up, with eager hands
Collecting and possessing. Happy birthday!
I don't recall if there was, at the center,
Some grand surprise or if, after unwinding,
The paper fluttered airily to its end.

PAINTERS,
MUSICIANS,
WRITERS

Bamboo

When the emotions are strong and one feels pent up, one should paint bamboo.   A PAINTER OF THE YÜAN DYNASTY

Light glazes the out-there. Therefore a sheet
Of paper is a world for human will.
As the plant grows, the brush begins its fleet
Exfoliations. Leaves break forth until
An emptiness that occupied the core
Of all that could be seen with a clear eye
Fills with the stems' strokes poised in ink before
The pale, undifferentiated sky.
Up from the root, up through the knots, design
Urges toward life; spontaneously, the air
Is charged with vigor; intricate shapes define
A grand simplicity. Now, everywhere
Leaves reaching out in loveliness obey
The painter, whose spent brush is put away.

Titian Makes Preliminary Studies for a Picture of Saint Sebastian

A thorn pricks as he reaches toward a rose.
A hemisphere of blood forms. It is pain
Here at a fingertip. His body knows
Its principles. He feels his muscles strain
When pulling on a cord—not in the arm
Alone, but chest, and thigh, and calf, and foot.
He senses how the sinewed tensions form.
He bends. The flesh hangs heavier at the gut.
His hand may now begin a martyr's death.
Sebastian twists where ropes loop to the stake.
The archers shoot. The artist hears his breath
Taken in gasps. Each line thickens to make
A tortured blackness as the saint is shown
With Titian's studied agony his own.

Rembrandt Prepares for a Walk along the Amstel River

Some days are for detail. An adventuring eye
Presents the house, the wagon with its load,
The boat, the windmill distant on the sky,
Each shrub and stalk, each rut etched in the road.
Others are inward days—the light in trees,
Not trees; not the horizon, but a wash
Of distance thinning on infinities;
Mind's arcs, and not the grasses of a marsh.
This day he gathers paper, brush, and pen
As he has done, now, countless times before,
Knowing the road that he will take again.
He feels, his hand unlatching the heavy door,
A rush of pleasure and possibility.
Then he walks out to see what he will see.

A Farmstead with a Hayrick and Weirs beside a Stream

When he was about forty-six, Rembrandt made several drawings of the same farm.

Perhaps it was the texture of the calm
That brought him back—the straight stakes of the weirs
Combing the stream; light blurring a tree's crown
Above a thick board wall; nets in the air's
Warm ruffle; and the hayrick, yellow and high,
Dense as the dwelling's thatch. Perhaps it was
The sense of an entire prosperity
Not got by owning, but bestowed—because
Here the clear eye could have, the pen could keep,
The terrace with its rail, the browsing cows,
The watery, reedy tufts beside the steep
Banks, the ducks, the whole of farm and house
And all beyond, even beyond the brink
Of space beginning at the edge of ink.

From Nature

Monet's wife, Camille, posed for each of the four figures in his life-sized
painting, "Women in the Garden."

He wished to put a window at the scene.
A trench was dug. The huge canvas could rise
Or lower as he painted, yet remain
Always at the level of his eyes.
His wife would pose—a distant left profile;
Then, closer, turning right to look at flowers;
Full faced, then, standing; seated, with a smile.
Daily he worked, and at predicted hours
So that the sun would angle as he willed.
He planned each shadow falling on a gown;
Raw colors touched the petals; quick strokes stilled
Occasional gusts of wind. When he was done,
He looked beyond the window's frame to see
A fragrant world, a friendly company.

The Tranquil Life

Never paint if you wish to live tranquilly.

COROT, TO A FRIEND

The most inviting landscape, where we say,
"Here we may rest and make this landscape ours,"
For him is apprehension. To convey
A moment of its meaning calls on powers
He sometimes doubts possessing. In his hand
The palette with its colored spots and smears
Seems to match nothing. On the easel's bland
And vacant canvas not a line appears
To guide him. While we gaze and shift our eyes,
Accumulating all there is to see,
His fuller sight begins to realize
A world brought into being anxiously,
Where structured shapes and contoured colors show
A calmer scene than any we could know.

Three Houses

Beethoven had three houses in which he was said to hide himself by turns.

    The artist hid within his infancy,
    Leaving behind the weather at the door,
    Leaving the view from windows. He would be
    In mother's arms, in father's arms, before
    A box of toys that opened with a click,
    A slight surprise each time. He hid in dreams
    Where he would be in fields where he could pick
    Wild buds from thorns, unharmed, or soar on beams
    Of sunlight, high and pure, above a land
    Astonished, with loud voices calling, "Ho!"
    He hid in worlds he did not understand,
    Only aware that his fate was to go
    From house to house until received inside
    A dwelling where he would not have to hide.

Chopin's Fantasy

*Today I finished the Fantasy. The weather is beautiful but I am sad
at heart — not that it matters.*   FROM A LETTER, 1841

Weather is always there, and yet his art
Requires its removal from the mind.
Sitting before the keyboard, sad at heart,
He tries a passage. Works it. Is resigned
To noting down, to going on, in spite
Of feeling distanced — alien — when the sound,
The soul, is fixed, and stares back, black on white,
Up from the voiceless page. Ideas come round
As minutes pass. The melodies return,
Now differing from those that had begun
The unpredicted journey that would earn
Their permanence. The Fantasy is done.
He rises toward the window while the day
Is lovely in its vanishing away.

A Way of Speaking

When Brahms was young, he tried to lower his strikingly high-pitched
voice by speaking hoarsely, which gave it an unpleasant sound.

> To speak was an embarrassment. To be
> Without expression was a kind of death.
> Others with natural felicity
> Made music with their words; his husky breath
> Was ugly noise, and no one wished to hear.
> But still he sensed a world of things to say —
> Communication for an inward ear
> Brought to attention in another way.
> He set about to find himself, to find
> The deepest root of impulse he could reach
> And bring it, note and rhythm, into mind,
> Making not merely individual speech
> But song that others would produce by choice,
> As though his was their purest, loveliest voice.

Scarlatti at the Cabin

He likes arriving. Jolting in the car
Along rough roadways, rhythms of the wheels
Thumping on stones remind him how we are
On solid ground. I feel the way he feels.

We stop knee-deep in grass. I see him look
With pleasure at the meadow sloping down
To the tall pine grove, and to Wadsworth Brook.
Listening closely, we detect the sound

Of water flowing. It is a surprise,
After I ask him if he wants to go
To the brook's lovely margin, when his eyes
Answer, "What we would see is what we know."

Upon a rise the one-room cabin stands,
Weathered and sunlit. As we near, our talk
Is the unspoken dialogue of friends.
We enter the small space, and I unlock

An elegant double-manual harpsichord
I'd made, and tuned especially for this day.
He smiles, and moves affectionately toward
The resonant instrument, and begins to play.

Rising in Music

1

The silence in the hall before the sound
Begins is as a darkness before light.
The mind brought to attentiveness has found
A will to fly but not a power of flight.

2

The singer draws a breath. A note
Is born into the air.
A trembling in the throat
Moves out into the expectant atmosphere,
From a small point enlarging everywhere.

3

Rising in music from our dailiness
We are made new. The body falls behind
The soaring thoughts whose patternings express
Our passionate and harmonious humankind.

4

Beyond the edges of the galaxies,
Where once resounded music of the spheres,
No music now is heard.
Still, in completed moments such as these,

An image of infinity appears
In melody and word,
While each one, listening here, attends
The hushing of a song that never ends.

A Commentary

On Horace's "Integer vitae" (*Odes*, I, xxii)

> If it were true, the truly righteous one
> Could walk unarmed into a dangerous wood,
> Assured that beasts will gorge on those whose sin
> Stinks, and not the guileless, or the good.
> If it were true, blank deserts could sustain
> The lover-poet's body when the heart
> Beats fervently with rhythms that the brain
> Will shape into the messages of art.
> If it were true . . . but Horace knew that lies
> Are the imagination's stock in trade;
> That nothing is revealed without disguise
> When a command for speech must be obeyed
> And all that one's deep sense of things can say
> Is: "I love. And a fierce wolf ran away."

The Poet's Horizons

Ah! How I would like to show you these boundless horizons.

COROT, DYING, TO A FRIEND

Beginning gold with grass dried in the sun
Smelling of summer, starting white with flowers
High on their stalks, the journey is begun
Attentively. The leaves will tell the hours
As light angles above them and their shade
Moves down the page, their trembling in the air
Blotting and mottling words and phrases made
For you. Beyond untended furrows where
Field poppies make their pinkish-red display,
The cows' tails flick, undoubtedly for flies,
And, at the valley's edge a mile away,
Particular trees engage the arching skies,
Putting an end to our infinity.
Could I but show you. Could I but let you see.

Genesis

The earth was without form, and void; and darkness was upon the face of the deep. And the Spirit of God moved upon the face of the waters.

GENESIS 1:2

What spirit moves upon the waters? Where
Do all its turbulent intentions tend?
When life is summoned from the void, is there
A patterning that life can comprehend?

In darkness seed is sown, and from the seed
The child comes forth, a spirit from the deep;
It cries, seeks steady light, and, with its need
Awakened, tires and falls away in sleep.

Yet when new day returns, the idea forms:
The day returns. With this perception, "Why,"
The child will question, "in a world that warms
From day to day, must spirit ever die?"

Years then become a turbulence of will,
Working within for ends always unknown,
Though each in ardor labors to fulfill
The secret destiny sensed as its own.

And while the years declare reality,
While destinies divide, some sinking down
To depths and darknesses as others see
Success in sunlight, riches in renown —

Though all move toward a mystery — the few
Who trace the solar patterns, who observe
The patterns their own passing lives renew,
Recording them in sound and color, serve

To grant to all the sense that spirit lives,
That here, beyond vicissitudes of place
And time, an everlasting spirit gives
A human face to the dark waters' face.

SHORT STORIES

Charles

Alice must gather flowers. In the field
She reaches through thick brambles and the snarls
Of spines to where the loveliest are concealed,
Then, beaming, runs and offers them to Charles.
Bradley is told to tame the stream. A pile
Of rocks is placed where it will brace a board.
The flow backs up behind it. With a smile,
He compliments himself and hurries toward
Charles, who sanctions all that happens here.
Throwing the bouquet down as if annoyed,
Charles kicks the dam just where it would appear
To be most solid, so it is destroyed.
Still Bradley, sullen, sets to work again,
And Alice binds her flowers in a chain.

The Road to Bethlehem in Song and Dance

There is no curtain at the end of the scenes. Instead young girls and boys dance to the tune of the Calypso carol and form a curtain. Thus, each scene flows smoothly into each other.

FROM THE PROGRAM NOTES FOR A NATIVITY PLAY PERFORMED IN ZAMBIA

Marina, as the Angel Gabriel,
Brings good news to Samantha, who portrays
Mary. She, with women at the well,
Joins the full choir in a hymn of praise.
After a tiring walk to Bethlehem
In Scene Two, after Pradeep, Mary's spouse,
Searches in vain for shelter at an inn,
They find a lowly stable for a house.
Young children dance to link the stories so
That nothing not alive will come between
These affirmations of new hope. And now
The boyish Wise Men enter, having seen
Surani and her three friends from afar—
Four beaconing lights, one cast as the Main Star.

The Dreamscape

I found her out there . . . I brought her here . . .

THOMAS HARDY

They both said they would love it. He was sure,
Because the northern air was his from birth,
And he had confidence that he could cure
Her thoughts of any other place on earth.
Therefore, while children came, and grew, his life
Was dedicated to the land, to build
Terrestrial paradise, so that his wife
Would come to find her every wish fulfilled.
Gardens were planted, marshes made a pond
Where fishes arced at evening. But one day
She asked, "Might we move southward?"—and a bond
Was broken, and the dream was swept away,
As though the waters every stream had fed
Were choked with algae, and the fish were dead.

On Their Deaths: An Older Couple

The peaches, with a month of steady sun,
Have ripened on the boughs. An attentive brood
Of sparrows learned its tunes, but is not done
With melody, at every dawn renewed.
Though skies grow bleak with cloud as I walk out
Into a world where they no longer are,
I do not let my mind darken with doubt
That they too reached a ripeness, and though far
From saying with the certainty of birds
That their songs are continuing through time,
I shape my thoughts of them around the words
That gather recollection into rhyme
As one assembles permanence — though pain
Comes with the gust of wind, the smell of rain.

Sisyphus's Pet Rock

I have my rock, my hill. So, every day
My task, though hard, is known. And as I roll
My rock, its weight seems always to convey
A certain satisfaction to the soul.
Near sunset-time, just before I can see
The highest point, I purposely let go.
My rock responds and, thanks to gravity,
Takes its own way back to the plain below.
I follow willingly, our duties done,
And grateful that another day's in store,
And glad to think my rock and I are one
In labor and in meaning. Surely, more
Is not to be expected; surely we
Will have our task throughout eternity.

Low Tide on Ile D'Yeu

Boats that bobbed in the bay lean on their chines
In a new world. A dark, luxuriant
Seaweed covers the squat rocks. Mooring lines
Droop to the sand from silent bows and slant
Away at angles — markings, as on Mars.
An artist marks his sketchbook, looking over
Low tide's landscape. Slowly, under stars
Emerging in the dusk, he will discover
Other figures — children gathering stones
Who call to parents on a distant ledge;
A couple walking slowly across dunes
Behind the beach; and, at the fading edge
Of water, in the last light, what must be
A person fishing, casting toward the sea.

FOUR SEQUENCES

WAR

The Disasters of War

After Goya

Not during, but just after, for a moment,
When he had lowered his sights, as from a distance
He saw himself, the center of the torment
Ebbing with blood from people whose resistance
Had, for a moment, awed him. They were finished,
He was finished for the afternoon.
He'd feared he'd see himself somehow diminished
By this performance, but he noticed soon
That everything was usual. The farm,
The fields, the family lying in the mud,
Had their correct proportions. No alarm
Need trouble him, though he resolved he would
Be reticent if anyone should ask
For explanations, or take him to task.

Play on a French Beach

The notice dated 1976
Says every animal must have a leash.
But no one seems to mind when balls and sticks
Send yapping dogs zigzagging down the beach
Toward Nazi bunkers built in the Second World War
That tilt on dunes eroded by the sea,
Or in between grim blocks, the footings for
A bridge, now gone, that reached artillery
Emplacements on an outcropping of ledge.
I look about, watching the dogs careen
At play, and notice numbers near the edge
Of one huge concrete slab, and see the scene
When, pouring done, as little children do,
A soldier traces 1942.

Touring

On June 10, 1944, the Nazis massacred the inhabitants of Oradour-sur-Glane and burned the entire town.

We locked the car in the lot, and with a shiver
Went into the martyred village where
A sign said, "Silence." Downward toward the river
We followed streets through mildest evening air.
We saw the post office — an empty shell,
A blackened bakery, the roofless shops,
Bent iron girders, twisted as in hell,
And murdering places at the trolley stops.
We saw an enameled ad for fire insurance,
The gutted church, memorial to the dead
Women and young burnt there in innocence.
We saw the graves. Then, in its shadowy bed,
We saw the Glane. So, with our touring done,
We drove home, toward the red ball of the sun.

"You Can't See Anything without a Flashlight"

The boy is disappointed. At the door
He turns back from the bunker where the men
Who manned the German guns in the Second World War
Once slept—perhaps had just awakened when
The bombs began, when friends began to die,
Blasted or buried; when, as they were taught,
They ran to train their bullets at a sky
Dropping disaster on the Pointe de Hoc.
Now, almost fifty years after that day,
The young arrive to see a sunny field
Of craters like the moon's, and find their way
To secret rooms. But nothing is revealed
Unless one brings a flashlight, or one brings
Some other light, to make sense of such things.

FOR A GERMAN SOLDIER

The New Recruit

He's young. Therefore his will can be controlled.
Sent with the new recruits onto a farm,
He fills the truck with all that it can hold—
Carrots, potatoes—noting with alarm
The band of skeletal laborers in a field
And, later, on the road, a mass of men
Crying out in hunger. He will yield,
And throw out food. He is beginning when
An angered officer rides up, whose whip
Flicks as he shouts: "Halt! Halt!" What has he done?
These men are starving. Staring at a lip
That spits the words, "These foreigners are scum!
Are enemies!" he feels a sudden fear
Numbing him, and almost barks, "Yes, Sir!"

As a Prisoner in Russia

A good job was beyond all human strength:
The orders were to dig potatoes where
The rows stretched to kilometers in length;
The prisoners were almost in despair.
"By dark!" a guard had snarled. So every man
Obeyed, and from the ground potatoes came
In multitudes — at first — but then began
The fateful gamble to survive, the game
Where prisoners stumbled forward bringing few
Of those now ripe for harvesting to light,
While they raced toward the field's end to be through
With day's impossible demand by night.
Fair work would have been willing. But they'd got
Their lives dug up, and what was left could rot.

Starting Over

"My sons could be my grandchildren." Before
He had fulfilled his youth, and found a wife,
The country's leaders sent him into war
And broke the hopeful pattern of his life.
One who survived — among so many dead,
So many like himself — he came home dazed
To learn the deep deceit of those who led
Him into horrors he himself had praised.
Dispirited and undermined, he passed
A dozen years of middle manhood sure
That when the world would end for him at last,
Death would be far easier to endure.
Though, then, he met a woman on a train,
And life began, and youth began again.

A VISIT TO NORWAY

Oslo

Here, trees spike into sun. Abruptly, hills
Rise to fall backward toward the frozen pole,
Buckling and creasing so salt water fills
The fjords far inland. From this point of view
Above the sunlit city, we control
The nearby landscape, mapping, pointing to
Known roads, known buildings, as if this could be
A diorama, set beside the sea.

Sculptures

The permanent children, bronze and kneeling where
They look across the mirroring pool toward tall
Fans of water jetting into air,
Say, in their metal way, no cycle should
Permit the sadness of a fountain's fall—
As though their youth was flesh, and understood
Our longing that this world could be retained
In cold months, when the pipes and pools are drained.

The Singer

Her voice above the quietly strummed guitar
Is thin and high. It is a song from France,
Of finding and of losing love. There are,
In the small room, the objects that proclaim
The life found here. Her eyes look up and glance
Along the walls. Each drawing in its frame —
Chagalls, Picassos — shimmers, as if through
Articulate color it was singing too.

The Widow's Apartment

They have the look of books no longer read—
As though the spines would crack, as though each page
Would flake or crumble. With her husband dead,
The oil portrait in its gilded frame
Seems like a relic from another age,
An age she enters nightly with the same
Bedside light going out. Life has begun
To winter, even with the midnight sun.

Bathers

At noon the traffic slows. A city fume
Rises through air warmed by the summer sun.
The parking spaces fill. Hungry for room
Along the solid shore that is a pledge
Of liberation, bathers one by one
Move out on smooth rocks to that very edge
Where Norway is a strength, an armored land
That needs no southern easiness of sand.

ON BASHO'S WAY

Traveler in Eternity

Yesterday, the funeral of a friend.
Three days ago, our summer garden tilled.
Now, with a hard month coming to an end,
The season's obligations are fulfilled.
So I begin my morning life once more,
Delighting to move on without delay
Into a world I've never known before,
Finding my way, following Basho's way.
New images may meet me on the road,
And meditations unexpectedly
May end with some new certainty bestowed
On this lone traveler in eternity.
　　The tuneful clock surprises me at noon,
　　Dreaming of distant waters, and a moon.

Tuneful chimes of the old clock,
Gong! Gong! But do not suppose
You can sing on without me.

Preparations

*I wanted to travel light, of course, but there were always certain things I could
not throw away.*   BASHO

Wanting to travel light, I tried to pare
The lists of what I thought I needed down.
No use for extra coats or shirts to share
Along the way, if journeying alone.
No use for more than one of anything —
A cup for wine or water, and a dish
For food: one fork, one knife. No need to bring
Additional gear, because it was my wish,
I thought, to go without a care. But when
I had my pack in order and the road
Opened before me, all seemed small. So then
I made new lists, glad to increase my load
   With things another might require one day,
   Gifts I would truly need, to give away.

   How will you lead us, Nadia,
   Into our future? Will sharp
   Barking hail new companions?

Departure

Shamed by the wind, moved by the cloud-streaked sky,
Roused up by Nadia's whimpering at the door,
I wonder, as I tell my past good-bye,
Who I will be when I am home once more.
My dog is ready. Looking to the north,
We find the poet's path, we see the way
Basho went, toward the far ends of the earth,
And start out—though my spirit's holiday
Is not entirely joyful, for the force
Of memory urges me to stay behind
With things long loved. Yet, having set our course,
We follow Basho's way, perhaps to find
    The diligent adventurer, not dead,
    Around the next bend in the road ahead.

From the waving hands of friends
Past hours, like birds departing,
Take flight at the fingers' ends.

Observations

We pass a cherry tree whose blossoms crowd
Into the vigorous gusts of warm spring air.
How far will we have journeyed when a loud
Music will say the birds are feasting there?
We reach a wide pond where I pause to gaze
At my clear image — until Nadia's tongue
Wrinkles my face in water. Are the days
Rippling away? Am I no longer young?
And there, ahead, the distant mountains rise,
Green and austere. How much time will have passed
Before we reach their summits and our eyes
Look toward the unimagined North at last?
   I feel the weight of years already gone,
   As Nadia barks, and pulls, and leads me on.

Aware of our departure,
Fish arc through seas of sunlight
To splash good-bye behind us.

An Avalanche Seen from the Road

The wrecked foundation dominates the view
From where we start, finding a pathway down
Between remains of rubbled walls and through
Split timbers, testing each unsettled stone
That seems triggered to send us on a slide
Into the gorge, where ice in the springtime melt
Shoved a whole household from the mountainside
Where, for a century, the family dwelt
Without so much as a rattled window, not
So great a trembling as a tree will make
Falling at a distance. At the spot
Where the last trace of wreckage lies, we take
    A turn, and come upon a beautiful
    Flow of water dropping into a pool.

Nadia bends to drink. Tadpoles
At a pool's warm edge, alarmed,
Dart into deeper waters.

At Midday

I did not wish to ride, so when the lord
Passed with his horses, I could wave him by
And go on walking. Suddenly I heard
The chattering magpies, harbingers of joy—
Then, even over the swishing of a stream,
The plucked notes of an instrument. I glanced
Into a clearing, shining after rain,
To see deer grazing. As the day advanced,
The mountain summits darkened into mist.
I knew my purpose. Pausing at a gate,
I found the lodge where I would be a guest.
A servant lit the way with lantern light
  And, as a courteous scholar greeted me,
  Moved about the room preparing tea.

  Nadia, do not nip the heels
  Of the lord's horse, or your head
  May be struck like a small gong!

Encountering the Painter

There is no mystery to the mountain, though
Weather transforms each image of a tree,
Each outline of a pinnacle, and so
The painter must discover what to see.
The rocks are rocks, the branches that extend
Beyond the cliffs are branches, but the scene
Is blurred in mist and fog as colors blend
Into a wash of gray and grayish green.
So while we watch the artist paint, and share
His wish to capture what the mountain is,
The shapes and textures alter as the air
Deprives the clearest sight of certainties,
    Though careful brushwork labors to convey
    The solid world within the shades of gray.

Oh Nadia, if the steep path
Is lost as we go onward,
It's your nose we will follow!

The Famous Mountain

Others crowd about us as we climb
The steps that trace the ridge of a ravine
Into the mists displacing tracks of time
Within the spectral groves of evergreen,
And on to heights where, though we talk or touch,
We draw into an inwardness and find
Our separate beings misting into such
A sense of sharing we become one mind
Where colors merge, where contours of the trees
Enlarge the rocks, where rocks shade into space
While bounds are passed into infinities
And we live perfect moments in a place
   Where lines dissolve, where distances draw near,
   And eyes that meet are luminously clear.

Look, Nadia, where the mountain
Is darkening. Our friends are
Preparing for the moonlight.

Arrival

So few more steps — the summit just ahead,
A freshened breeze dispersing bands of mist —
Yet with each step a sense of almost dread
Assails me strangely, and my feet resist
Arrival, though I do arrive where light
From a full moon unveils reality
As, from this lonely pinnacle of night,
The myth of Nature is made plain to me.
I see ravines that only darkness fills,
And seas whose luminous gleams seduce the eye;
I see, along the planet's rim, the hills
That close the borders of infinity,
    While here I see no others to extend
    A hand to, or be close to, or befriend.

Nadia looks strangely at me,
Perplexed at my distraction.
Her tail wags, "I am with you."

Kingdoms

The kingdoms of the world surround me now,
Though from this mountain's height the sharpest eye
Can see no farther than straight lines allow
Before they come to nothing in the sky.
Although I might descend and make my way
On wider roads where others have pursued
Distinction and acclaim, my soul says, "Stay
Upon this path. Go on in solitude."
Perhaps a friendly spirit has a hand
In guiding fortunate travelers like me
To heights that help them finally understand
The structure of a happy destiny
    That finds fulfillment in the smallest things,
    And leaves the kingdoms of the world to kings.

A hive says bees are home here.
See, Nadia, where they gather
Their sweetnesses together.

In an Upland

How long have we been going? Nadia's sniff
At rocks and stumps now seems perfunctory—
As if she's losing confidence, as if
Her inner self is saddening, like me.
The little stream that runs beside the way,
Which could be cheerful, gurgling over stone,
No longer has original things to say
And gives one message in a monotone:
My flow is downward. Even while the sky
Presents new pictures in its clouds, while trees
Create new music when a wind goes by,
My mind swirls backward into memories
    As, with the stream's, imagination's flow
    Falls helplessly onto the rocks below.

Sunlight silvers the water.
On Nadia's tongue a luster
Is scooped up in her drinking.

Apprehensions at the Barrier Gate

Here, for the first time, my mind was able to gain a certain balance and
composure, no longer a victim to pestering anxiety.

BASHO, AT THE CHECKING STATION OF SHIRAKAWA

Here at midsummer's checkpoint I must pause
To wonder, is this way the way for me?
Basho was happy going on, because
Each step diminished his anxiety.
But memories of what is left behind,
Of gentler scenes, yet scenes that are my own,
Come flooding, with each further step, to mind,
And make me long for landscapes I have known.
The images arise of friends long dear
Who have been strength, and hope, for decades past;
I see each one with apprehensive fear
That death one day will seek us out at last.
    Across a barrier, lands are always new,
    But here I am, and I will not pass through.

Nadia, do you hear echoes?
Is this why you gaze backward
And whimper for a first time?

A Happy Retreat from Shirakawa

Farewell, companion, brother to my rhyme.
When starting out together with my dog
I hoped that in a recreated time
We two would have continual dialogue
While I was venturing with you toward a North
Where life could be felt newly, so that then
Restored imagination would bring forth
New vision, and a world made fresh again.
But halted here, at the first barrier gate,
Where ancient accents tuned for your own land
Give you a voice, I now must meditate
In my own world, if I will understand
    My own particular journey. We must go
    Our separate ways, then, friend. Farewell, Basho.

When he first stooped to pat you,
Nadia, and rub your shoulder,
His eyes were mist, as mine are.

Return

The door moves on its hinges. In the hall
We enter home's familiar atmosphere.
I ask, was journeying needful after all,
When all we went in search of had been here?
We greet the friends attending our return
With Nadia's barks and waggings, while each word
Of hope and welcome signifies concern
For both of us, though now more clearly heard.
We tell of somber hours, of pleasant days
With lengthy roads to walk and hills to climb,
And of brief moments when the mind would raise
Itself, and see into our life and time—
    Not Basho's life and time—though we could say
    His spirit had been ours along the way.

Lying across the threshold
Of the closed door, Nadia sleeps.
A moon is in her sleeping.

Notes

"On Basho's Way": Matsuo Basho (1644–94) is one of Japan's renowned poets. Among his most widely known works are his travel diaries, where narrative passages alternate with haiku. The prose and the poetry recreate each excursion's hardships and pleasures, and the meditations that they inspired.

Basho's most famous journey, from Edo (now Tokyo) to the mysterious northern provinces, was begun in the spring of 1689 and lasted about six months. During that time, he visited places made famous by earlier poets and wrote about the celebrated shrines, remarkable natural scenes, and various people he encountered. He called his record of this adventure *The Narrow Road to the Far North*.

Acknowledgments

A number of poems in this book appeared originally in the following publications, to whose editors grateful acknowledgment is made:

The American Scholar: "Rembrandt Prepares for a Walk along the Amstel River" and "A Farmstead with a Hayrick and Weirs beside a Stream"

Boulevard: "Titian Makes Preliminary Studies for a Picture of Saint Sebastian"

The Formalist: "Preparations"

The Maine Scholar: "Bamboo"

Musicians, a chapbook published by Aralia Press: "Three Houses," "A Way of Speaking," and "Scarlatti at the Cabin"

Pivot: "Her Handbag" and "Step by Step"

Poetry: "Play on a French Beach," "The Tranquil Life," and "Sisyphus's Pet Rock"

Portland Review of the Arts: "A Commentary"

Sparrow: "From Nature"

The Texas Review: "Charles," formerly titled "Children at Play"

wordplay: "The Dreamscape," "On Their Deaths: An Older Couple," and "Low Tide on Ile D'Yeu"

"Play on a French Beach" also appeared in the 1987 edition of *Anthology of Magazine Verse and Yearbook of American Poetry*. "A Farmstead with a Hayrick and Weirs beside a Stream" also appeared in *Kennebec*.

"Rising in Music" was written for the composer and singer Bruce
Fithian, who set it for harp, oboe, and tenor for performance at
the inauguration of the Corthell Concert Hall at the University of
Southern Maine on September 19, 1986.

I am once again deeply indebted to John Irwin for his generous
assistance with selecting poems for a new book. Likewise, I am
grateful to Dana Gioia for expert advice and friendship over
many years. To Anne Whitmore, for her thoughtful advice about
the manuscript, and to all of the other helpful people at the
Johns Hopkins University Press, my thanks.

THOMAS CARPER's poems and translations have appeared in *Poetry, Sparrow, The Dark Horse,* and other national and international journals, as well as in several textbooks. He and his wife, Janet, live in southern Maine.

Poetry Titles in the Series

John Hollander, *"Blue Wine" and Other Poems*

Robert Pack, *Walking to My Name: New and Selected Poems*

Philip Dacey, *The Boy under the Bed*

Wyatt Prunty, *The Times Between*

Barry Spacks, *Spacks Street: New and Selected Poems*

Gibbons Ruark, *Keeping Company*

David St. John, *Hush*

Wyatt Prunty, *What Women Know, What Men Believe*

Adrien Stoutenberg, *Land of Superior Mirages: New and Selected Poems*

John Hollander, *In Time and Place*

Charles Martin, *Steal the Bacon*

John Bricuth, *The Heisenberg Variations*

Tom Disch, *Yes, Let's: New and Selected Poems*

Wyatt Prunty, *Balance as Belief*

Tom Disch, *Dark Verses and Light*

Thomas Carper, *Fiddle Lane*

Emily Grosholz, *Eden*

X. J. Kennedy, *Dark Horses*

Wyatt Prunty, *The Run of the House*

Robert Phillips, *Breakdown Lane*

Vicki Hearne, *The Parts of Light*

Timothy Steele, *The Color Wheel*

Josephine Jacobsen, *In the Crevice of Time: New and Collected Poems*

Thomas Carper, *From Nature*